RAYS OF TRUTH

Poems on Islam

Ayesha bint Mahmood

The Islamic Foundation

ISBN 0 86037 263 4

General Editors:
M. Manazir Ahsan and **Anwar Cara**

Rays of Truth: Poems on Islam

Author: **Ayesha bint Mahmood**
Design and Layout: **Abdullah Nait Attia**

Published by
The Islamic Foundation
Markfield Dawah Centre
Ratby Lane, Markfield
Leicester LE67 9RN,
United Kingdom.

Quran House
P.O. Box 30611
Nairobi,
Kenya.

P.M.B. 3193
Kano,
Nigeria.

Printed by Renault Printing Co. Ltd., Birmingham, England B44 8BS.

MUSLIM CHILDREN'S LIBRARY

An Introduction

Here is a new series of books, but with a difference, for children of all ages. Published by the Islamic Foundation, the Muslim Children's Library has been produced to provide young people with something they cannot perhaps find anywhere else.

Most of today's children's books aim only to entertain and inform or to teach some necessary skills, but not to develop the inner and moral resources. Entertainment and skills by themselves impart nothing of value to life unless a child is also helped to discover deeper meaning in himself and the world around him. Yet there is no place in them for God, Who alone gives meaning to life and the universe, nor for the divine guidance brought by His prophets, following which can alone ensure an integrated development of the total personality.

Such books, in fact, rob young people of access to true knowledge. They give them no unchanging standards of right and wrong, nor any incentives to live by what is right and refrain from what is wrong. The result is that all too often the young enter adult life in a state of social alienation and bewilderment, unable to cope with the seemingly unlimited choices of the world around them. The situation is especially devastating for the Muslim child as he may grow up cut off from his culture and values.

The Muslim Children's Library aspires to remedy this deficiency by showing children the deeper meaning of life and the world around them; by pointing them along paths leading to an integrated development of all aspects of their personality; by helping to give them the capacity to cope with the complexities of their world, both personal and social; by opening vistas into a world extending far beyond this life; and, to a Muslim child especially, by providing a fresh and strong faith, a dynamic commitment, an indelible sense of identity, a throbbing yearning and an urge to struggle, all rooted in Islam. The books aim to help a child anchor his development on the rock of divine guidance, and to understand himself and relate to himself and others in just and meaningful ways. They relate directly to his soul and

3

intellect, to his emotions and imagination, to his motives and desires, to his anxieties and hopes - indeed, to every aspect of his fragile, but potentially rich personality. At the same time it is recognized that for a book to hold a child's attention, he must enjoy reading it; it should therefore arouse his curiosity and entertain him as well. The style, the language, the illustrations and the production of the books are all geared to this goal. They provide moral education, but not through sermons or ethical abstractions.

Although these books are based entirely on Islamic teachings and the vast Muslim heritage, they should be of equal interest and value to all children, whatever their country or creed; for Islam is a universal religion, the natural path.

Adults, too, may find much of use in them. In particular, Muslim parents and teachers will find that they provide what they have for so long been so badly needing. The books will include texts of the Qur'ān, the *Sunnah* and other basic sources and teachings of Islam, as well as history, stories and anecdotes for supplementary reading. The books are presented with full colour illustrations keeping in view the limitations set by Islam.

We invite parents and teachers to use these books in homes and classrooms, at breakfast tables and bedsides and encourage children to derive maximum benefit from them. At the same time their greatly valued observations and suggestions are highly welcome.

To the young reader we say: You hold in your hands books which may be entirely different from those you have been reading till now, but we sincerely hope you will enjoy them; try, through these books, to understand yourself, your life, your experiences and the universe around you. They will open before your eyes new paths and models in life that you will be curious to explore and find exciting and rewarding to follow. May God be with you forever.

May Allah bless with His mercy and acceptance our humble contribution to the urgent and gigantic task of producing books for a new generation of children, a task which we have undertaken in all humility and hope.

CONTENTS

FOREWORD

Although a number of books in English have been produced by Muslims for children and young people, both in the East and the West, nothing much of significance has been contributed in the field of Islamic poetry. Poems, in any language, are a powerful medium to convey ideas in a convincing, moving and lively style which not only captures the imagination of the reader but provides him a unique pleasure not usually obtained through prose writings. Unlike Islamic languages, the English language, which has now assumed a prominent place among Muslims, particularly those living in the West, does not contain anything substantial on Islamic poetry. The reason for this is easy to discern. Not only is it difficult to write poems, there is hardly any proper training and encouragement for young Muslim writers to devote their talents and energy in the field.

The present collection, *Rays of Truth: Poems on Islam*, is a laudable effort by a young Muslim writer to fill the gap in a very humble way. These poems, centred around the noble teachings of Islam and conveyed in the language of gentle rhyme, embody a diversity of themes ranging from prayer and fasting, seeking Allah's guidance and pleasure to seeking knowledge, sharing brotherhood and increasing one's love and devotion to Allah. It is hoped that not only the young but also people of a mature age, from both Muslim and non-Muslim backgrounds will enjoy reading these poems and, perhaps through them, discover a greater sense of purpose in life.

I am grateful to my colleagues and friends, both in and outside the Foundation, for their generous help in reading the manuscript, offering valuable suggestions, and seeing this small book through the press. I am particularly indebted to Dr. A.R. Kidwai, Brothers Sarwar Rija, Anwar Cara, Mrs. Asima Qureshi and Mr. E.R. Fox for their help in reading, editing and finalizing the manuscript. I am also indebted to the author for offering the poems to us and ungrudgingly accepting our suggestions for change and improvement.

May Allah, *subhānahū wata'ālā*, reward them all and make this publication a source of inspiration and guidance for all, in particular the younger generation.

Rabi' al-Awwal 1417   **M. Manazir Ahsan**
July 1996   Director General

THERE IS NO GOD BUT ALLAH

Allah! Indeed there is no god but You
Your glorious creation bears witness to this Truth
So help us to testify, O Exalted Being!
Your Existence gives our life its meaning

Allah! Indeed there is no god save Him
Lord! Help us to enlighten our hearts that are dim
And train us as servants of Your Good Will
O Allah! Your Goodness, in our hearts, please fill

Allah! Indeed no King rules but You
Show us the purity in all things true
And drape us in piety and make our souls tender
O Allah! Help us lovingly surrender

Allah! Indeed, You alone deserve Praise
Grant us, O Generous! Your bounty always
And O Most Kind! Grant us this delight
Your Pleasure, each day and each night.

WE SEEK REFUGE IN ALLAH

I seek refuge in You O Allah!
From eyes that are not restrained
and from a tongue that is not tamed
I seek refuge in You O Allah!
From a heart that is complacent
and from a mood that is not patient
I seek refuge in You O Allah!
From a soul that is not grateful
and from a thought that is not lawful
I seek refuge in You O Allah!
From a limb that is not humble
and from conviction that begins to stumble
I seek refuge in You O Allah!
From hoarding every pence
and from slowness in obedience
I seek refuge in You O Allah!

8

From love of material life
and from ignorance of Eternal Life
I seek refuge in You O Allah!
From the trials of life and death
and from the punishment of the grave
I seek refuge in You O Allah!
From the trial of Ad-Dajjāl
and from the torment of the blaze
Grant me wisdom, O Most High!
And understanding and strength
Grant me fortitude, O Magnificent!
And humility to repent
Grant me light, O Most Merciful!
To penetrate my heart
Grant me Your Love O Creator!
For the Greatest Thou art.

WE SEEK REFUGE FROM HELLFIRE

Hurl him headlong into the pit of Fire!
Never from evil did he part nor tire
But roaming the earth and causing man pain
Hurting humanity without any shame!

Cast him headlong into the burning Flame!
Never did he call on, or praise Allah's Name
But laughing and mocking every man of truth
Careless in manhood and heedless in youth

Throw him headlong into the piercing Blaze!
He who rejected his Creator always
Who stood protecting his deeds - untrue
If goodness approached, he would try to undo

Seize the denier of Allah the One!
He whose past life was reckless fun
Who failed to cleanse his darkened heart
Ever-ready, from Allah's Will, to depart...

The torturous Fire
will burn the hardened sinner!
Who disbelieved in Allah
and thought he was the winner!
But not the fearful servant
who yearned for Allah and paid heed
Safety from the Fire
for him is guaranteed,
Because he pleased our Maker
the wrong, he chose to leave
On him no fear nor sorrow
Nor harm nor will he grieve
O servants! Seek refuge in Allah!
And Hellfire makes this plea
It says 'For all of Your servants, Lord!
Grant refuge to them from me'!

BELOVED MESSENGER OF ALLAH ﷺ

Although I never saw your face
So beautiful, bestowed with grace
My heart doth yearn to be like you
In thoughts and hopes and actions too
You loved the children and the old
And gave your heart to every soul
You nursed the sick and served the poor
And fed the hungry at your door
You loved the creatures - tame and wild
And comforted the orphan child
You bid men peace, cared for the youth
God's Messenger in truth

So with devotion I do read
Your life of which I try to lead
No deed is mine except is yours

My prayers upon you ever pour
The good-tidings you brought to me
And for mankind, we'll ever be
In humble praise of our Good Lord
For bringing His great Message forth

Now to my Lord I turn to pray
'O Allah! Your last Messenger's way
Lit the earth whereso he went
This truthful, gentle soul You sent
O Allah! Your last Messenger's life
Was the perfect sacrifice
To bring Your people to Your Garden
In hope he prayed for our pardon
Guiding, steady and forbearing
Patient with us for not caring
O Allah! Our love for him cannot sever
Peace and blessings on Muḥammad for ever.'

13

ALĀT IS OUR SUSTENANCE

Ṣalāt is our armour
that guards from harm and sin
Ṣalāt is our medicine
that soothes our aching limb
Ṣalāt is our vehicle
that carries us through life
Ṣalāt is our soldier
that fights for good and right
Ṣalāt is our garment
that covers and conceals
Ṣalāt is our therapy
that lifts our mood and heals
Ṣalāt is our pillow
that gives us rest and peace
Ṣalāt is our sustenance
that satisfies our needs

Ṣalāt is our teacher
that guides to all things pure
Ṣalāt is our shelter
that makes our hearts secure
Ṣalāt is our lantern
that lights up our Straight Way
Ṣalāt is our good-tidings
that helps us through our day
Ṣalāt is our vitamin
that strengthens our Īmān
Ṣalāt is our treasure
full of spiritual charm
Ṣalāt is our victory
a crown upon our heart
And blessings come to every servant
who loves to pray Ṣalāt.

15

SLEEPY EYES!

O sleepy head!
Do not make haste for bed
But after Ṣalāt ʿIshā'
Crave for even more Thawāb
And stand with me for a night prayer

O sleepy eyes!
Do not fail to realize
As your lids start to close
Your last breath may be near - just suppose!
Better then, to stand for a night prayer

O sleepy soul!
What burdens do you hold?
This longing for respite
To sleep all through the night
Your night prayer will revive you untold

O weary self!
You are bestowed with good health
You are passing through life
With wealth and keen sight
Owe Allah a little thanks then this night

O supple bed and carrier!
You stand as a barrier
Between me and my Lord
Your comfort stirs discord
Do not kindle your warm welcome for me!

I have preferred the hard floor
Therein lies comfort much more
On the dusty hard ground
Allah's Nearness is found
How blessed is the nightly prostration!

AL-ḤAMDULILLĀH

As I rise each day
Al-Ḥamdulillāh I say
As I put on my dress
Al-Ḥamdulillāh I express
As I fill my empty plate
Al-Ḥamdulillāh I state
As I make ready to strive
Al-Ḥamdulillāh for another day alive
As I hear the birds sing
Al-Ḥamdulillāh for the melody they bring
As I watch the sun rise
Al-Ḥamdulillāh for my eyes
As I wash in the stream
Al-Ḥamdulillāh I am clean
As I pray my Ṣalāt
Al-Ḥamdulillāh for the best start
As I share my gifts with neighbours
Al-Ḥamdulillāh for Allah's favours
As I delight with my family
Al-Ḥamdulillāh for their care of me
As I pray for forgiveness
Al-Ḥamdulillāh for deliverance
As I open the Qur'ān
Al-Ḥamdulillāh for my Īmān
As I understand and take heed
Al-Ḥamdulillāh, Al-Ḥamdulillāh
For all the good I receive.

GUIDED

Praise be to You my Lord for these limbs
Praise be to You my Lord for this mind
Praise be to You my Lord for the Truth
Glory be to Allah Most Kind

How pure is Your Light that encompaseth me
The Light of the Heavens and the Earth
You guided this lost soul to enter Islam
A passage of purity and worth

You cast away the root of my crippling illness
And sowed the seed of Īmān
You tore away the pages of my impiety
And placed before me Al-Qur'ān

So Praise be to You my Lord for this jewel
Praise be to You my Lord for this crown
Praise be to You my Lord for this pearl
Glory be to Allah for the treasure I have found!

Although I still mourn my ingratitude O Allah!
I beg of You a humble request
O Most Merciful grant me the shelter
Of Your Nearness and there let me rest.

BLESSINGS

Allah Ta'ālā gives me all that is good
He guides me to fulfil the tasks that I should
By His Great Bounty, I work and I pray
Through His Vast Mercy I rise every day
My bread and my water come from His table
He nourishes my body and then makes me able
When I have a difficulty, He puts it at bay
When I am in pain, He takes it away
He gives me protection from evil, from wrong
He transforms my weakness and makes me strong
Allah is Kind and Compassionate and True
He created mankind equal - everyone - me and you
Islam is our brotherhood, a life that is best
Our Path to Allah is truly the greatest
My gifts are many, all beautiful indeed
I say 'Praise be to Allah - You I will please'
For all of my life, to Allah I pray
'Inspire me to worship Your Name night and day
And give me more strength to follow Your Dīn
And love me as Your servant - Āmīn.'

HEARTS AND LIMBS

For You, O Allah! with these eyes do we see
For You, with these ears, do we hear
Pour on us blessings and bounty our Lord
And bring to us, Your Countenance, near

For You, O Allah! with these hands do we grasp
For You, with these feet do we walk
Grant us the movement of righteousness our Lord
And on our tongue let the truth talk

For You, O Allah! we discipline our soul
For You, our spirit do we mould
Grant us the fragrance of true Īmān our Lord
And make our conviction more bold

For You, O Allah! do we live this short life
For You, we shall one day depart
Grant us a goodly departure our Lord
And take to You a forgiven heart.

WONDROUS WORLD!

O world full of wonders!
O world full of might!
Approach not this naive soul
Tempt not me, with delight
For your plentiful ease
Will most certainly cease
And put out your temporary light

O world full of glitter!
O world full of gold!
Get away from my presence
Before you are told
For your enchanting call
Will not lead me to fall
In my hand, a strong rope, I hold

O world full of comfort!
O world full of charm!
I see you as a dungeon
Disguising your harm
But amidst your tribulation
Is a gateway to salvation
Allah's Straight Path
- of purity and calm

O world! Be no distraction
From meaningful action
This young slave seeks something more true
So leave me alone peacefully
My Lord - I shall serve willingly
O Next Life! My soul yearns for you.

FORTUNATE IS HE

Fortunate is he
Who remembers Allah abundantly
Worldly distractions cannot mildly sway
His thoughts of Allah and Judgement Day

Righteous is he
Who prostrates to Him as though Him he can see
Whose deeds do not spring without Bismillāh
Fulfilling his tasks with perfect Taqwā

Devout is he
Who makes supplication to Allah intensely
Whose heart fills with mercy, is tender and kind
His gaze on the Ākhirah, this world behind

Prosperous is he
Who spends of his wealth on the poor and needy
Who speaks a kind word to his kin and his neighbour
Ever-grateful and indebted for Allah's Favours

Guided is he
Who attends to Ṣalāt with punctuality
And extra ʿIbādah, Tahajjud he prays
For Allah's Pleasure and Nearness he craves

God-fearing is he
Who contemplates death, takes provision early
Whose limbs start to shiver as he reflects his demise
And tears stain his face over wasted sacrifice

Blessed be the pious
Who sing Allah's Praises fervently, tireless
Blessed be His slaves
Allah's Mercy and Blessings be upon them, always.

SSALĀMU 'ALAIKUM

Familiar faces we often greet
Exchanging dialogue while we meet
But as we gesture, respond or smile
Before we speak, just think a while

Welcome not with words unrewarding
'Hello', 'Good day', 'Good evening', 'Good morning'
But choose to radiate peace and calm
Offer a warm exchange of 'Salām!'

'And peace on you' - comes the reply
Will bond our kinship and strengthen our tie
To those unknown, do not hesitate
We are one family in Islamic faith

Allah's servants of the sky
The Angels extend this humble reply
And our acceptance into Grace
Yields 'Salām' - a blessed fate

So give glad tidings with words serene
Spread the blessings of 'peace' - our Dīn
And relish the good of this healing balm
And wish all our brothers and sisters 'Salām'.

EARTH'S BED

O earth! the bed within you, is today lying bare
But one day this stranger will occupy you
So embrace my bones gently
- with tender compassion
And do not become my enemy

O earth! I have lived and experienced some life
But never turned away from your memory
Your silent call beckons
- and severs my laughter
And your stillness has never deserted me

O earth! Allah knows when I must keep company with you
The day my blanket is your soil
So expand your narrowness for this fearful entrant
And shield from me all of your toil

This traveller will return to the dust she was made from
To face an eternal new life
O grave! prepare for me a pillow of comfort
And shine onto me, your welcoming light.

BROTHERS AND SISTERS IN FAITH

For all of my brothers and sisters in faith
For all those who, from the plate of Truth, taste
For all who, for their salvation they run
For all who surrender to Allah the One
For all who lift up their hands in duʿāʾ
For all who lower their limbs in Ṣalāt
For all who suffer hunger in fast
For all who love to purify their hearts
For all who open their arms to the poor
For all who greet with warm smiles and more
For all who humble themselves with fear
For all who beg for forgiveness in tears
For all who testify to His Presence, sure
For all who glorify our Maker All-Pure
For all Allah's servants, this small prayer have I
'Lord! Cloak us with mercy, esteem in Your Eyes
And O Source of Comfort! pour peace from above
And swell us with good works and actions You love
And O Most Merciful, fulfil our dream
And grant us rest in Your Garden - Āmīn.'

DEDICATION

Gentle Lord! And Sovereign and King
I dedicate to You everything
Lord! Not a single day goes by
That I do not sincerely try
To become Your faithful slave
So yesterday, my heart I gave
To Your Will and perfect Word
As if my ears had truly heard
The sweetest call to something pure
There stood greatness at my door
And so I opened up my heart
And led it along my yearning path
And kindly let it prove to me
That Your Will, Lord, is best for me

My eyes have only learnt to see
The beauty that has always been
Embedded in my living soul
Truth is my heart's mould
And certainly You are on my side
Making smooth life's trying ride
So now my Lord each day I pray
'Keep all Your slaves on Your right way
For we all dearly long to be
So loved by You eternally
And O Allah! with joy we bring
Our souls surrendered as Muslim.'

OUR HOPE IS ALLAH

As the darkness of the night
spreads her silent cloak
Some assurance finds my heart
a glimmer of past hope
As the sound of shelling and gunfire
for a moment, ceases
We gather our Shahīd
our heroes slain to pieces
Our dreams are carried forward
by the Mujāhidīn left behind
No less dedicated to martyrdom
serving our Lord, Divine
My home is Bosnia, Chechnya
Palestine and Kashmir
Where the world does not care
for my blood spilled and fear
You say I am the enemy
seeking confrontation!
I am Muslim! A slave of Allah
With Him, lies my dedication
In our barren homeland
true justice is forlorn
We innocent are despised

our Muslim honour is torn
Shame on you, the enemy soldier
grinning and feeling joy
You hear my heartbeat throbbing
then painfully you destroy
Mercilessly roaming
heedless to warnings - dire
No thought of Allah's punishment
of the eternal Fire!
O our Lord! Please save us
our young, innocent children
Save our fathers and our mothers
save our men and women
Our hearts cannot bear to cry
Nor save our daughters from perverted eyes
Our existence is haunted
our land full of strife
We live in a world that cuts like a knife
But before O people! you spit on me
You'll never snatch my gift of belief
A guiding shield till we have conquered
My hope never left me **Allāhu Akbar!**

 MANKIND!

O mankind!
What seduces us from Allah Most Gracious?
A love of this life, of wealth and of easiness?
Be mindful of seduction
Of alluring corruption
It can shake our faith
and bring our destruction
Let us repent! Why aren't we humble?
Know that Allah is Most Merciful

O people!
What distracts us from Allah Most Kind?
A pocket full of gold and a selfish mind
With true faith, from evil, we can surely depart
Seek help through patient perseverance and Ṣalāt
Then wait for reward with humble anticipation
Know that Allah is our Source of Celebration.

O humanity!
What keeps us from·thanking the Most High?
Which of our Lord's blessings would we deny?
Have we not sight when others are deprived?
Have we not water that tumbles from the sky?
And we have children and wealth and food
Let us Praise Allah and show our gratitude

O men!
Remember Allah and double success, nay more!
Islam is a life prosperous, unlike one before
Purity of faith and soul we shall gain
And spiritual happiness and joy and no pain
If sweetest delights, our hearts long to taste
Surrender to Allah the Giver of Faith

O servants!
Live by a Guidance most honourable
Be strong in faith and steadfast not gullible
Acquire the beauty and wisdom of the Qur'ān
Enrich our souls and expel the Shaiṭān
Behold! A new beginning, brings Light perfect
Sheds peace and tranquillity in this life and the Next
A glorious ray of hope, a source of our Īmān
Comes from the beauty of Al-Islam!

Slaves of Allah!
Reflect with your gift of wisdom
Turn to your Maker, vast is His Kingdom
Believe in the Truth and secure your fate
Perfect the submission, bow down and prostrate
Success will reach you, no longer afar
Crown your prosperity - declare 'My Lord is Allah'
And be a witness to mankind, pronounce the Shahādah:
'I bear witness that no god exists but Allah and Muḥammad is His Servant and Messenger'

ALLAH'S GUEST

Allah's House is today my destiny
To the Kaʿbah and the blessed city
To which I turn my face in prayer
But today I travel and journey there
Small world! Behind I gladly leave you
Your worldly comfort I give no thought to
I trek forward determined to strive
Ready to climb the mountains to arrive
Though my hands are bare and empty
My heart is full of Allah's Bounty
And patience, from Allah, I humbly request
To be my friend in this life's test
For each Muslim must undertake
The sacred pilgrimage for Allah's sake
This duty is our invitation
From Allah, to show our dedication
There bows a beautiful congregation
Mankind, together in supplication
And equal is every colour and person
In Islam no race is chosen...

Then after the Ḥajj is over
And we have gone away
Make duʿā' to Allah to take us back some day
And after the Ḥajj is finished
And we are home to rest
Give Praise and thanks to Allah
Who honoured us as His guest.

KNOWLEDGE IS...

Knowledge is an apple tree
Wisdom is to pick her fruit
Knowledge is a gallant sword
Wisdom is to slay Ṭāghūt
Knowledge is a waterfall
Wisdom is to cleanse
Knowledge is to know your neighbour
Wisdom is to befriend
Knowledge is a summer flower
Wisdom is her scent
Knowledge is to seek forgiveness
Wisdom is to repent
Knowledge is a shining star
Wisdom is her light
Knowledge is the freedom struggle
Wisdom is to fight
Knowledge is Divine Decree
Wisdom is to trust in fate
Knowledge is to raise our hands
Wisdom is to supplicate
Knowledge is a swelling plant
Wisdom is her seed
Knowledge is the Book, Qur'ān
Wisdom is to read
Knowledge is an ivory pearl
Wisdom is her charm
Knowledge is the certain Truth
Wisdom is Islam.

STRANGER ON A TRAIN

As you gaze across to me
Your searching eyes are questioning me
'How is it you live?' You say
'Do you trek a straight pathway?
With Whom do you daily plead?
Why this Book you always read?
And the dress you women wear!
Why this scarf upon your hair?
In your palm is there some power?
Why then supplicate each hour?
What then, do you claim to share?
For world justice do you care?
Tell me! Speak what is right
What then is your plight?'

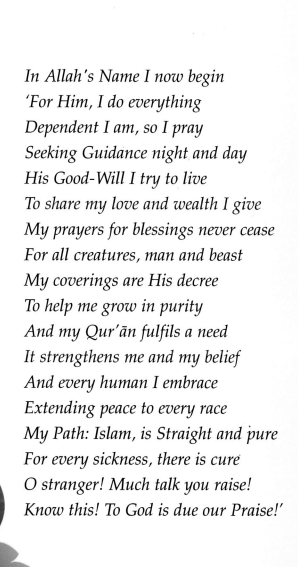

In Allah's Name I now begin
'For Him, I do everything
Dependent I am, so I pray
Seeking Guidance night and day
His Good-Will I try to live
To share my love and wealth I give
My prayers for blessings never cease
For all creatures, man and beast
My coverings are His decree
To help me grow in purity
And my Qur'ān fulfils a need
It strengthens me and my belief
And every human I embrace
Extending peace to every race
My Path: Islam, is Straight and pure
For every sickness, there is cure
O stranger! Much talk you raise!
Know this! To God is due our Praise!'

I AM A BIRD

I am a bird with outstretched wings
I go flying high above all things
Into the clouds my body soars
To softly depart from heavenly doors
Swift is my movement in timely motion
But I am the 'toil' in the thinking man's 'potion'
For man does observe but he cannot explain
He gazes above for answers in vain
How do I rise without visible strings?
A miracle, he confesses are my two wings
And then every morn. I wake with no fill
But when the day sets, I am nourished, yet still
He thinks I have no conscience
I tell you I have knowledge!

I will lift the veil from your blind eye
And tell you O people! that I am a sign
To him who searches for life's things - plainer
I tell you I have a Glorious Sustainer
The King He is, of all of the sky
The answer to your troubling 'why?'
I work and I live in humble service
I am created like you, for purpose, in earnest
To Praise our Creator, and worship our Lord
Together we must live in harmony, not discord
So listen O mankind! to this humble bird
Take flight to Allah's Word!

WISE WORDS

With this pen I pick up to write
With this hand I may have to fight
With this cup I lift up to drink
With this book I open to think
With this morsel I lift to devour
With this seed I plant a young flower
With this couch I rest on to dream
With flowing water I wash to be clean
With this cloth I cover my bareness
With true knowledge I gain an awareness
With this coin I spend from my purse
With this medicine, my pain, I can nurse
But guiding voices are calling each day
These simple life's tasks have wisdom and say
'O scribe! Will your pen print the names of your Lord?
O soldier! Will your hand strike for Allah, your sword?
O you who thirsts! Will you drink liquid pure?
O you with wisdom! On whom knowledge, do you pour?
O you who hungers! Will Ḥalāl food you serve?
O keen worker! For Allah do you earn?
O restful heart! Do you praise Allah in ease?
O cloth merchant! Is it pure, the dress you weave?
O wealthy soul! For the poor, does your wealth pile?
O you who heals! Do you honour the unborn child?
O you who washes! Are your limbs wet with Wuḍū'?
O slave of Allah! Be mindful of all you do!'

I WISH I WERE A SNOWFLAKE

My soul cannot rejoice
For within me, an inner voice
Reminds me of all I have done
And all I am failing to do
To leave me alone it may never
Throw rocks at my heart it may forever
And grip this frail self like a vice!
O I wish I were a snowflake
- on a warm summer's day
that melted peacefully away

What have I to do with this world?
As I begin its journey, it ends
As I begin to dream, it fades
I bring the cup of life to my lips but it chokes me
And then do I find Allah's Face!
This soul cannot recount the good it has done

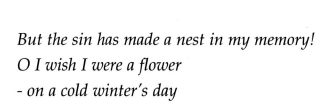

But the sin has made a nest in my memory!
O I wish I were a flower
- on a cold winter's day
that a strong wind scattered away

One Day I will stand before the Lord of the Worlds
One Day my soul will stand unclothed
Will my deed scrolls be pleasing
to Allah All-Seeing?
And a good account
will they proudly show?
The answers - they haunt me
As I recall my spent energies
O I fear what they reveal!
But true is Allah's Mercy
Flowing forth abundantly
In surer hope, my torn soul I heal.

DEAR FRIEND...

How beautiful do our grand oak trees
Sway peacefully in the morning breeze!
How radiant do our sun's rays glow!
Dear friend, will you kindly observe
Our Righteous Maker Who deserves
Our praises, for all things He sees

How pure is our flowing water!
That tumbles from the highest quarter
How delicate is our falling white snow
Dear friend, kindly contemplate
The wonders at your earthly gate
And resist not our Creator but follow

How glorious is our deep blue ocean!
A bottomless bed of salt and sweet portions
How colourful are our fishes that swim

Dear friend, kindly heed advice
And make a little sacrifice
And dedicate your heart unto Him

How cheerful is the gentle melody!
Full of praise and peaceful glory
Sweet conversation from our birds of song
Dear friend, kindly realize
Our Gracious Lord above the skies
And remember, to Him, we belong

The silvery stars do twinkle at night
And light up the heavens all glittering bright
Do you see friend, how our universe displays
All the clear and graceful signs
Of a Magnificent Lord, Divine
He is Allah so Praise Him, always.

A SPECIAL ʿĪD GIFT

Before the celebrations duly start
Remember those distant but near to our heart
Whose ʿĪd al-Aḍḥā holds little activity
But hardship substitutes their festivity
Our pleasures and comforts may not reach all
For on their faces, gentle tears still fall
And while our cooking pots brew with plenty
The needy long to fill their stomachs - empty
Who carry their sorrow, barely alive
Their pain is their luggage, their will - to survive
So in setting the table, make room for one extra
And welcome the hungry, the lonely, the beggar
ʿĪd is a reminder of their poor state
In sharing our gifts, their poverty, we alleviate
So during the sacrifice do not utter 'for me'!
But save a kind portion for the struggling family
And give Praise to Allah, and duʿā' for each family
May Allah bless us with the gifts of Qurbānī.

FORGIVE ME!

I can only break down and cry
I am drifting - true guidance is passing me by
Faith tackles my faithless heart
I climb life's ladder but it is slippery to cling to
My soul is empty, nothing to give to
A burning desire to change my ill state
I see a Straight Path but I hesitate
Recalling my life, a game in full play
I hope for longer than temporary stay!
How many sacrifices I will not make!
But then I am sealing the lid to my fate
A place is ready, with punishment - cruel
The sinner's dwelling is Fire, man - fuel
This reality plays on my conscience
Yet my debility conquers my good sense
But I search for the Truth in you
The sincere believer, blessed with virtue
Hopeful and humble, you are serving Him well
Focused and attentive, insecurity expelled
How lucky you seem, a picture of peace
Truth and direction for you, a release
Give me a piece of your sweetness I long
Show me the True way again I was wrong
To Him whom I pour out my heart faithfully
Surely hears and accepts my overdue plea
All the waste, all the weeping - to Islam I flee
The only path to salvation! May Allah forgive me!

45

CHILD'S WISH

My dear big sisters you are to me
My closest friends and family
And dear big brothers you have a part
Inside my home and near my heart
Though young I am
My bones are small
I wish to tell you something - all
I wish to see the greatest signs
That Allah kindly gives mankind
I wish to plant my growing feet
On the Path of joy and peace
I wish to grow with Islamic conscience
And know my Creator's Love and Patience
I wish to learn those humble tasks
And do the things that Allah asks

I wish to act on how to best
Help my parents and give them rest
My food and water, I wish to share
With other children because I care
And for my neighbours I wish to try
To be their friend and bring them smiles
So brothers and sisters teach me please
Pour into my heart your expertise
And train me all I need to know
To strive into the world I go
And O Allah! I pray to You
To guide me and my Ummah too
And on You let us all depend
Respond O Lord! My Best Friend.

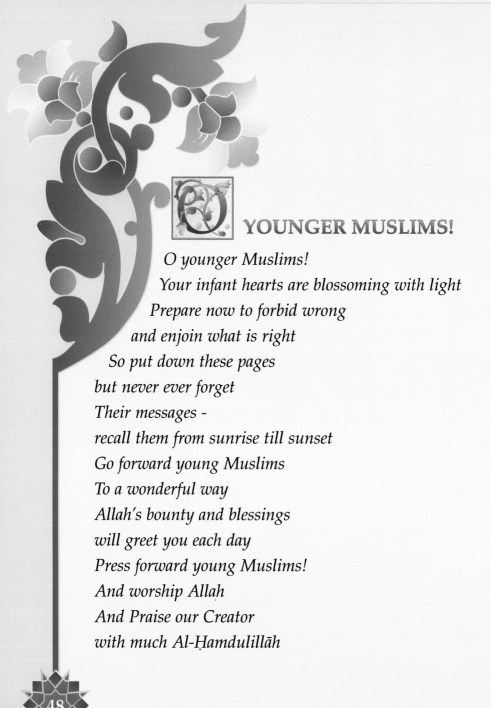

O YOUNGER MUSLIMS!

O younger Muslims!
Your infant hearts are blossoming with light
Prepare now to forbid wrong
and enjoin what is right
So put down these pages
but never ever forget
Their messages -
recall them from sunrise till sunset
Go forward young Muslims
To a wonderful way
Allah's bounty and blessings
will greet you each day
Press forward young Muslims!
And worship Allah
And Praise our Creator
with much Al-Ḥamdulillāh

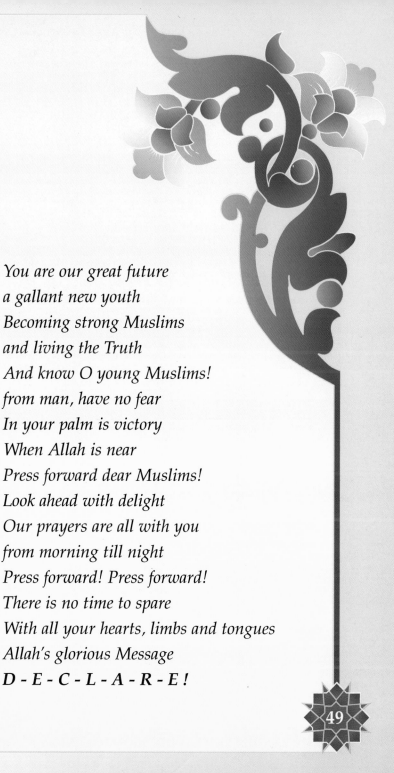

You are our great future
a gallant new youth
Becoming strong Muslims
and living the Truth
And know O young Muslims!
from man, have no fear
In your palm is victory
When Allah is near
Press forward dear Muslims!
Look ahead with delight
Our prayers are all with you
from morning till night
Press forward! Press forward!
There is no time to spare
With all your hearts, limbs and tongues
Allah's glorious Message
D - E - C - L - A - R - E !

WHAT CAN WE LOSE?

Inside my mind's tunnel, is darkness
I tread with careful tip-toes
And try to justify my misgivings
But fear all that You know

My tongue invents more excuses
For me, it is temporary solace
But soon I fear that my soul will declare
The root of all of my malice

My life does yearn for direction
This road is leading me nowhere
The steps I take are dark and crooked
I sometimes feel life is unfair

Unfair or am I misguided?
I have a free spirit to choose
Upon my shoulders rests a decision
If I take good, can I lose?

My mind's tunnel seems less darker
Once I begin to fight
My heart can feel a little sparkle
Like someone giving me light

My mind's eye can see a straight opening
A light that invites to the Truth
It extends me her gentle and welcoming hand
And now I shall never refuse.

THEIR GUNS DO ROAR

O my Lord! Their guns do roar
While tears of grief my eyes do pour
My brother, father, lying still
Slain for bowing to Your Will

O my Lord! My home they seize
While I pray upon my knees
My mother's covered flesh they tore
And raped for being pure

O my Lord! My sons they steal
Your soldiers on the battlefield
Left to rot in dungeon halls
My grieving heart upon You, calls

O my Lord! My eyes doth see
A vision! Faces beckoning me
Amidst tall thrones of pearls and silk
In Springs of wine and Fountains of milk!

O Kind Lord! My life, accept
For You I struggled, to You I wept
But now You willeth my departure
To Paradise O slave! Forever after!

PRAYING FOR A BETTER TOMORROW

Torment grows while we spill our tears
O dear Muslims!
Perhaps Allah we do not fear!
Tribulation is with us
And more rising sorrow
Let us pray for a better tomorrow

Tragedy overtakes us
Our heart is suffocating
Remedies are shallow
No action but debating
Unfair opinions offer unfair conclusions
Let us pray for a better solution

Our future is tainted
And our troubles are thickening
Our light was once bright
But now dim and flickering
But promises from Allah of joy and sweet laughter
Let us pray for a better Hereafter

Our life is continuing with ever more pain
Dear servants of Allah!
We are punished without shame
But hold fast to Allah, pray this decision
Serve Allah in total submission.

53

GLOSSARY

Ad-Dajjāl: Literally a 'cheat'.

Ākhirah: The Hereafter.

Al-Ḥamdulillāh: Praise be to Allah.

Allāhu Akbar: Allah is the Greatest.

Al-Islām: Muslims' way of life approved by Allah.

Āmīn: Amen.

Assalāmu ᶜAlaikum: Muslims' greeting, meaning 'Peace be on you'.

Bismillāh: In the name of Allah.

Dīn: Religion, covering all aspects of life.

Duᶜā': Supplication.

Ḥajj: Pilgrimage to Makkah.

Ḥalāl: Permitted, e.g. Ḥalāl food.

ᶜIbādah: Worship in a ritual sense, but all good actions are an act of worship.

ᶜĪd: Festival.

ᶜĪd al-Aḍḥā: Festival of sacrifice celebrated by Muslims who do not go for the Ḥajj or pilgrimage to Makkah.

ᶜĪd al-Fiṭr: Festival marking the end of Ramaḍān.

Īmān: Faith, conviction.

ᶜIshā': The fifth and last prayer performed in the night.

Kaᶜbah: The House of Allah - in Makkah, towards which Muslims turn for prayer.

Muḥammad: The last Prophet sent by Allah.

Mujāhidīn: Sing. Mujāhid, who struggles in the way of Allah.

Qur'ān: Literally, reading. The last Divine Revelation of Allah granted to the Prophet Muḥammad ﷺ

Qurbānī: Sacrifice (of animal during ʿĪd al-Aḍḥā festival).

Salām: Literally, peace, but means the Muslim greeting.

Ṣalāt: The ritual prayer offered five times a day.

Shahādah: Testimony - declaration of faith in the Oneness of Allah and the Prophethood of Muḥammad ﷺ

Shahīd: Martyr.

Shaiṭān: Satan.

Taʿālā: Exalted is He (Allah).

Ṭāghūt: Arrogant, Satan or any other leader/person who defies Allah.

Tahajjud: Optional late-night prayer.

Taqwā: Being conscious of Allah.

Thawāb: Reward.

Ummah: The Muslim community.

Wuḍū': Ritual washing (ablution) before prayers.

ﷺ: Stands for 'Ṣallal-Lāhu ʿalayhi wa-sallam', which means Allah's blessings and peace be upon him (Muḥammad).